Play On

Play On

Sandra Diersch

James Lorimer & Company Ltd., Publishers
Toronto

© 2004 Sandra Diersch

James Lorimer & Company Ltd. acknowledges the support of the Ontario Arts Council. We acknowledge the support of the Government of Canada through the Book Publishing Industry Development Program (BPIDP) for our publishing activities. We acknowledge the support of the Canada Council for the Arts for our publishing program. We acknowledge the support of the Government of Ontario through the Ontario Media Development Corporation's Ontario Book Initiative.

Cover illustration: Steven Murray

The Canada Council | Le Conseil des Arts
for the Arts | du Canada

ONTARIO ARTS COUNCIL
CONSEIL DES ARTS DE L'ONTARIO

National Library of Canada Cataloguing in Publication

Diersch, Sandra
 Play on / Sandra Diersch.

(Sports stories ; 73)
ISBN 1-55028-857-1 (bound).   ISBN 1-55028-856-3 (pbk.)

I. Title. II. Series: Sports stories (Toronto, Ont.); 73.

PS8557.I385P53 2004   jC813'.54   C2004-904671-3

James Lorimer & Company Ltd.,   Distributed in the United States by:
Publishers   Orca Book Publishers
35 Britain Street   P.O. Box 468
Toronto, Ontario   Custer, WA USA
M5A 1R7   98240-0468
www.lorimer.ca

Printed and bound in Canada.

Contents

For Paul, Rosamund, and Cailen
with love
and in memory of Lilah Finlay.

Special thanks to Ellen for her
valuable suggestions.

1

The Smell of Spring

Alecia Parker blew on her hands as she waited on the field for the opening kick. She noted that the other players looked extremely large, and pretty confident. Her teammates kept their feet moving, and hands tucked under their arms for warmth. The mid-March morning was cold and windy — not at all spring-like.

"Let's go Burrards!" rallied the captain, Laurie Chen. All around her came the the other girls' spirited cries.

The opposing team, the Crusaders, won the toss and took the opening kick. Their centre passed the ball to the left-winger before Trina, a gritty Burrard forward, tackled her and got possession. Trina sidestepped two wingers and moved the ball back over centre, then fired a sharp pass to Alecia. Alecia fought to control the ball.

"Open!" screamed Lexi.

Alecia frowned as she looked for her teammate. Finally she found her, about twenty feet from the Crusaders' goal.

"Pass it!" Lexi shouted again, but Alecia's hesitation cost her a clear kick. Two huge Crusaders boxed her in. She lost the ball and took a bruise to her shin in the process.

Laurie battled another tall forward for the ball. She juggled it between her feet before kicking it behind to Lexi. A cheer rose

from the Burrards' bench as the team hurried down the field
with the ball.

"Pass, Lexi!" Marnie, a Burard forward, called from the left
of the net.

Lexi fired a hard shot to Marnie, who kicked it at the net.
The goalkeeper dove, and for a long second her whole body
hung suspended above the ground. Alecia shook her head in
frustration as the keeper came down with a thud, the ball cradled safely in her arms. The goalkeeper looked dazed as she got
to her feet and threw the ball back into play.

The Crusaders were quick, but couldn't get the ball out of
their own end. Laurie snagged a poor pass and aimed it at Lexi.

"I'm open, Lex!" Alecia waved her arms over her head.

Lexi's pass came to her in a perfect arc. Alecia braced herself for the impact. She bounced the ball off her head, directing
it toward the net. Laurie trapped it with her chest and kicked it
between the posts.

Laurie ran to Alecia in triumph and threw her arms around
her. "That was amazing! Did you see what happened? I thought
for sure Brenda was going to pick it off!" She hugged Alecia
excitedly. As they jumped up and down the other girls sur-
rounded them, slapping them on the back and high-fiving each
other.

"Great playing, Laurie! You too, Alecia." Lexi smacked her
on the back.

"Thanks Lexi."

"You might want to work on those headers, though. With a
little more push behind it, that ball could have gone in without
Laurie's kick."

Alecia scowled at Lexi. Since her arrival in January, Lexi
had been correcting the other players, criticizing their play —
trying to coach. It drove everyone crazy. And worse, she got

mad if anyone tried to tell her anything. Alecia opened her mouth to reply but Laurie beat her to it.

"A goal is a goal," Laurie snapped. "Besides, Alecia used to just let the ball land on the ground beside her!"

Alecia flushed as her friends laughed and Lexi looked confused. "It was just a suggestion."

"No coaching during a game, Lex," Laurie warned.

"You won't let me say anything at practice either, though."

"You're right, I won't!"

Alecia scanned the sidelines looking for her dad. Finally she found him, near the Burrards' bench, his coach's clipboard in one hand and whistle around his neck. He caught her eye and smiled, giving her a thumbs-up. Alecia grinned and waved back as she positioned herself for the kick.

* * *

The game ended before lunch — just ahead of the rolling black clouds coming in from the east. Alecia took a big drink from her water bottle and wiped her hand through her bangs. She couldn't wait for her usual bath and hot lunch. She tucked her shin pads and cleats in her bag and let out a long breath.

Despite the approaching storm and cool temperature, a smell of spring filled their Vancouver neighbourhood. The cherry and plum trees were in bloom — their fragile pink and white blossoms scenting the air — and crocuses were up in the gardens. Alecia shivered as she slipped into her jacket. Suddenly she felt a hand pat her back.

"Good game today, Leesh."

"Thanks, Jeremy." Alecia felt a warm glow spread through her. "Did Mom come at all?"

"Yes — she said to tell you she was proud of the header. She also saw the goal, but had to leave to help Grandma with some shopping."

"I hope she remembers to pick up some more milk — we're out. *Some* of us drink too much with our cookies."

"Hey," Jeremy protested as they headed off the field together, "I can't help it. Blame Mr. Christie."

Alecia laughed and smacked his arm. Alecia's friend Anne Leung was waiting near the parking lot.

"Are you walking home with Anne, then?" Jeremy asked.

"Yeah, is that okay?"

"Sure." He gave her a hug, waved at Anne and headed for the car. "See you at home."

Jeremy Parker had been in Alecia's life for ten years, but he'd only become her father recently when the adoption papers had arrived from Victoria.

For some reason Alecia had worried things might change once the adoption was finalized, but everything felt the same. He was still lovable old Jeremy, the guy who helped her with math, coached her soccer team, joked around with her and was always beating her at Scrabble. They were as close as ever.

"Nice header, Leesh." Anne smiled as Alecia approached.

"Thanks. We had a few good plays."

"Well, I thought you all did *awesome*. Karen was amazing! Only two goals and what, five saves? She didn't look nervous at all. She's really settled in as keeper since she took over from Stacie last month."

"I know. We don't even miss Stacie that much."

"I still can't believe Stacie quit because you guys wanted Lexi to stay on the team. Do you think she'll change her mind?" Anne asked.

"No. I did. Or I hoped she would. But now I don't think she'll ever come back. She can't stand Lexi." Alecia shrugged and took another long swallow from her water bottle, emptying it. She tucked the bottle in her bag and zipped it closed.

"Is Lexi really that bad though? She's a great athlete. I'd love to play with her — she's so fast!"

"She's pretty annoying," Alecia said slowly. "But it helps knowing how bad things are at home. You know what I mean? I don't think I'd be a nice person if my dad didn't want me around."

Anne didn't answer. For several minutes the two friends walked along quietly together. When Anne spoke again she changed the subject completely.

"That's great about you and Jeremy," she said.

"Yeah."

"What happens next? Will you have a big party to celebrate?"

"Mom, Jeremy and I talked about having a fancy dinner. But we haven't decided yet," Alecia said, adjusting the bag on her shoulder.

"Are you still calling him Jeremy? Aren't you going to call him Dad?"

"It's hard. I still think of Peter Sheffield as my father and Jeremy has always just been Jeremy." Alecia made a face and shrugged.

"But your birth dad died almost ten years ago, Leesh. You don't even remember calling him Dad."

Alecia didn't need reminding. Still, deciding to let Jeremy adopt her had been a hard decision. She and her mother had talked about it a lot. Alecia knew her dad would want them both to move on with their lives. Jeremy adopting her was part of that. So was calling him Dad.

"Jeremy says I will when I'm ready."

"What about your last name? Are you going to be Parker

now, like your mom?" Anne asked.

"Yes. I definitely want to take Jeremy's last name. Hyphen-ating Sheffield and Parker would be long and annoying, don't you think? Besides, Parker is easier to spell."

Anne nodded thoughtfully. "It must feel strange to have a new name all of a sudden. I mean, you've been Sheffield for nearly fourteen years."

"Yeah, I know," Alecia said slowly. "I'll probably forget sometimes too. At least we're a real family now that we all have the same name. Know what I mean? I feel more like Jeremy's daughter now that I have his name." Alecia shrugged. It was hard to put her feelings into words but Anne seemed to know what she meant and Alecia was glad to end the conversation.

Their friends, Connor Stevens and Laurie were walking ahead with Trevor Lunden. Alecia slowed her pace. Trevor had moved across the street from the Stevens family in February, but Alecia didn't particularly like him.

"Alecia!" Connor called, turning towards the two girls, "Trevor thinks you looked good out there today!"

Trevor blushed and made a face at Connor. He pushed his glasses up his nose self-consciously. "You have a good team," he muttered. "Some of your passes are sloppy though."

Alecia bristled at his criticism but Laurie answered. "You're right! But we're one of the best teams in the league right now. And we're going to take the championship next month!"

"Laurie, don't jinx us!" Alecia cried.

"I wish I hadn't quit last fall," Anne said wistfully. "I'd love to go all the way in the championships."

Alecia squeezed her friend's elbow. "You're coming back in September, Annie," she said firmly. "We need your speed on offense."

"Yeah," Laurie added. "And your great heading skill.

Although Alecia is giving you a run for your money …"

"You play soccer?" Trevor asked Anne.

"She's a great soccer player," Laurie told him. "She was the Burrards' captain until she had to quit last fall."

"She's also the reason Alecia started playing," Connor added. "Not that she always wanted to. I remember a time when Alecia wanted to quit too! But her dad wouldn't let her … right Leesh?"

"Are you finished giving my life story?" Alecia asked, embarrassed in front of Trevor. It was true — she had tried to quit with Anne. She'd thought that she only played because of her friend. But now she was glad that Jeremy had encouraged her to see it through, because she was becoming a good player and liked the game.

2

Appearance

"Try this colour — 'berry splash' — it'll look good with your green eyes and blonde hair." Monica looked critically at the small compact she held in her hand and then at Alecia's face. Then she nodded in satisfaction. "This lip gloss goes with it, too."

Alecia looked at herself in the mirror. She almost didn't recognize herself; her fair lashes were long and black and a thick smear of violet shadow ran across her eyelids.

"Are you sure I need this much?" she asked.

"Absolutely! It makes your face stand out. I'm taking a course on makeup application. My mom says it's important to know how to use this stuff properly."

"What about you, Annie?"

"I don't know, I don't think my parents would like it." Anne picked up a compact then dropped it back on the bed. She sighed heavily and fell back against the pillows, eyes closed.

"One of these days you're going to have to start standing up for yourself, Annie. I mean we are almost fourteen, and sooner or later our parents have to start letting us make our own decisions."

"Monica, you don't know my parents. They never let me do anything! Well, my dad doesn't anyway. He's determined to ruin my life," Anne grumbled.

Alecia looked in surprise at her friend. She put down the lip gloss and crawled across the pile of makeup to sit beside Anne.

"What's going on, Annie? Did you have another fight with your dad?"

Anne sighed in frustration. "It's just, well, Tyler asked me to go to the movies with him, but —"

"Really?"

"You're kidding!"

"When?"

"After school. We were walking home and he just asked."

"What did you say?" Monica was up on her knees, her darkened eyes bright with excitement.

"What could I say? I told him that my dad won't let me go on dates."

"You didn't really say that, did you? You'll scare him off Annie! You have to say yes — then figure out a way to go!"

"Monica, shut up!" Alecia glared at her. "Annie, don't listen to her. What did Tyler say?"

"He said we'd figure something out! He's such a nice guy."

"Can't you just tell your dad a whole bunch of us are going out together and include Tyler in the group?" Alecia suggested.

Anne swung her legs over the side of the bed and stood up, looking more confident. "Good idea. I feel like such a baby about this."

"You aren't a baby. But it'll work, you'll see."

* * *

On Wednesdays Mrs. Parker usually went to the gym after work, so Alecia was surprised to see her mother's car in the driveway when she got home. She let herself in the front door, kicked off her shoes and wandered into the kitchen.

Her mother was sitting at the kitchen table with a cup of tea and a magazine.

"You're home early," Alecia said.

"I think I'm coming down with something. I thought I'd pass on the workout. How was your day?"

"Okay. Same old."

Alecia sat down beside her mom and poured herself a cup of tea. She closed her eyes and leaned back in the chair.

"What's that all over your face?"

Alecia grimaced, sitting up again. She had intended to take the makeup off before she left Monica's, but forgot once they had started talking about the upcoming band concert.

"Makeup," she muttered, touching her eyelid.

"I see that, yes. But what is it doing on your face? You don't wear makeup."

"Monica is taking lessons on how to use it. She offered to teach me."

"Has she had many lessons so far?"

Alecia caught the sarcasm behind her mother's words and tensed. She hated it when her mom got that tone in her voice. "I don't know," she said slowly. "She just said these colours went well with my hair and eyes."

"Well, you have way too much on. Besides, you don't need makeup. You're beautiful without it."

"You're my mother, you're supposed to say stuff like that. But Monica says people notice you more when you wear make-up."

"What sort of people do you want to notice you?" Her mother took her cup to the sink.

She was still dressed in her skirt and jacket from work. When she turned again to face her, Alecia noticed her mother's own makeup. You could hardly tell she had any on. Her lips were pink and her eyelashes darkened with mascara, but that was it. Alecia blushed at the thought of her own face.

"I don't know, guys, I guess …"

"Guys."

"I don't know! Cripes, what's with the inquisition?"

She banged her mug down on the table, sloshing tea over the side.

"Don't yell at me, please."

"Well, quit bugging me then! It's just makeup! Everyone else wears it …"

"Watch your tone, Alecia! I don't care who else is wearing makeup; I don't think you need to."

"What's the big deal? It's not like I want to start smoking or anything. I didn't come home with a tattoo or a belly button ring."

Alecia stood up and grabbed her bag. Why hadn't she just remembered to take the stupid stuff off before she'd left Monica's?

"You aren't allowed to do those things, either," her mom said with a smile.

Alecia refused to smile in return. As she headed out of the room, her mother called after her.

"I have people coming over tomorrow night for a meeting and I'd like you to vacuum and dust the living room please."

"Can't you do it?" Alecia whined. "I've got homework and soccer." She knocked her pack against the door, but stopped when her mother frowned.

"Yes, you do. So I guess you'll have to get busy as soon as you get home from school, then, won't you? I'd like you to help around here a bit more than you do."

Alecia scowled, but kept her mouth shut as she banged out

of the room and up the stairs.

The next afternoon, Alecia stayed at school waiting for Anne and it was after four by the time she got home. She grabbed a snack, then headed upstairs to tackle the history assignment her teacher had thrown at them that day. She was still working on it when her mother arrived an hour later.

Mrs. Parker poked her head in the bedroom door to say hi. "How was your day?" she asked. "How did your math quiz go?"

"Fine — not as hard as I thought it would be."

"That's good. Don't forget about the vacuuming and dusting, please."

"I'll try."

"I'm going to the store to pick up some things. And I've put a casserole in the oven. We'll eat when I get back so would you also please set the table?"

"Fine, whatever."

Alecia heard the garage door open and then her mother's car backing down the driveway. She glanced at her watch. Jeremy would be home soon, and they would leave for soccer in an hour. She had plenty of time to finish her schoolwork and tackle the vacuuming.

Once she had finished her homework, Alecia went downstairs to set the table. She realized she was starving as the warm, spicy smell of her mother's casserole hit her nose. Jeremy came in, looking tired and grumpy.

"Where's your mother?"

"She had to get some things."

"I'm going to change and wash up. Are you ready for practice? We have to leave here as soon as we're done eating."

"Why?"

"One of the league officials is coming to discuss some

things with me. I need to see him before the girls get there. Be ready to go, please."

"I will be, chill out."

"Alecia ..."

"Sorry." She finished setting the table and ran back upstairs to change into her soccer clothes.

"Did you do the vacuuming and dusting?" Alecia's mom asked, serving dinner minutes later.

"No, I couldn't. I had tons of homework."

"I asked you three times! Well, you can do it before you go to soccer."

"I have to leave in ten minutes," Jeremy reminded her.

"Then I guess Alecia will be walking to practice tonight."

"Walking! It's *half a mile* and it's almost dark!"

Her mother took a bite of dinner. She chewed slowly before she answered. "I asked you to do something and you didn't do it."

"That's so unfair! I was doing my homework!"

"I told you yesterday I wanted it done. I don't want to hear any more about it, Alecia."

"It's not my fault Jeremy has to leave early." Alecia looked at Jeremy, but he only shrugged at her.

"I said not another word! You had all afternoon to vacuum and do your homework. You need to manage your time more efficiently."

Her parents got up and went their separate ways, Jeremy out to practice and her mother up to her room. Alecia finished eating in furious silence, and then went looking for the vacuum.

3

A Poor Showing

Saturday was wet and cool, but despite the weather everyone was pumped when they arrived at the field. Even though the Wolverines were a tough team with a good record, the Burrards were ready to go.

"Hey Alecia, you all set for this?" Karen asked as she put on her cleats. The other girls were milling around, waiting for their game against the Wolverines to start.

"Yeah. Hey, how's your leg?" Alecia asked.

Karen grimaced and rubbed the spot on her thigh where one of Laurie's killer shots had left a nasty welt. "It's still really sore."

"You'll be fine. Laurie won't shoot on you today!" Alecia grinned reassuringly.

The Wolverines started strong, with all their best players out first. The opposing centre won the toss and began play with a hard pass to her right. Her teammate caught the ball and dribbled it up the right side of the field. Rianne caught up with her and, with some fancy footwork, stole the ball away. Immediately the Wolverine centre was on top of her, digging for the ball.

"Pass it, Rianne!" Alecia moved into position behind them. Rianne tried, but the centre was all over her. They fought for several seconds until the centre shot her foot out and kicked the ball away.

The Wolverine charged back down the field toward Karen. The Burrards were caught unprepared for the sudden shift, and had to scramble into position. Laurie, Lexi and Allison picked her up before she got within striking range, but she took a shot anyway. The ball went rolling out of bounds.

Allison caught the throw in and started up field, the centre and two other Wolverines hard on her heels. She passed to Alecia at centre but Alecia was in an awkward position and passed it back. She groaned as a Wolverine picked it off.

Play turned back toward the Burrards' net. Three forwards were hot on the Wolverine's tail, but Nancy and Rianne were on the far side of the field, having anticipated Laurie moving the ball away from their net. They scrambled to get back in position.

"Get her!" Laurie cried. "What are you doing? Stay with the play you guys!"

The Wolverine midfielder dribbled the ball a few feet then passed back to the centre, who dribbled in close to the net unheeded and tried a shot on goal from a bad angle. Karen dove for it and just missed. The Burrards groaned as it rolled into the net behind her and lay in the corner.

"Concentrate on the game, Burrards," Jeremy advised from the sidelines. He made some player changes and play resumed.

Partway through the second half, the ref called back a Burrards goal when the Wolverines complained about interference. There was a loud chorus of booing from the stands, and Jeremy ran onto the field.

"What the heck was that, Ref?" he complained.

"Your player tripped the girl with the ball," replied the ref flatly.

"You've got to be kidding," Jeremy argued. "You call that tripping? How many times did they do the same or worse to my girls and you ignored it!"

The Burrards stood watching. They hadn't seen Jeremy get this upset before. But he was right — it wasn't fair. The ref was missing tons of calls against the Wolverines.

"Return to your bench, Coach, or you'll be asked to leave the field."

Jeremy and the referee stared at each other. Alecia knew her dad would go back to the sidelines — he was always teaching good sportsmanship. Sure enough, a second later, he returned to his position.

But the Burrards never managed to get things on track and the game ended with the Wolverines winning 3–0. The Burrards left the field quietly — heads down, shoulders slumped. There was no post-game chat, no high fives. They gathered around Jeremy at the bench.

"Sorry everyone, I'm not playing very well," Karen said as she sunk onto the bench. She looked totally defeated.

"It's not your fault," Jeremy told her, eyeing everyone else. "You can't defend a net all by yourself. What was going on in defence?"

The girls didn't reply. Most of them were looking at the ground, digging their feet into the dirt. Jeremy rubbed his hand across his forehead.

"Where was your focus today?" he asked. "You weren't working as a team. I know there were some bad calls but you've got to let those go and move forward. That's enough. Go home and we'll talk more at Tuesday's practice."

* * *

"Hi! What are you doing here?" Alecia called out as she opened the front door Monday morning. Connor and Laurie stood waiting for her at the end of the driveway, backpacks slung over their shoulders.

"I had to drop something off for my mom," Laurie explained as they started down the sidewalk. "So we decided to meet you."

"What did you do after the game on Saturday?" Alecia asked.

"Connor and I went to a movie Saturday night. Then we tried that new gelato place by the theatre — the one with over a hundred flavours."

As Laurie and Connor talked about the movie, Alecia's usual sense of discomfort began washing over her. When she was alone with Connor, things were the way they'd always been: easy, relaxed, and familiar. And at soccer she got along fine with Laurie, although they weren't exactly friends. But being with the two of them together was like trying to join two different puzzle pieces that just didn't fit.

"How 'bout you, Leesh?" Connor was asking, jabbing her in the side to get her attention. "Earth to Alecia …"

"Oh, me? Nothing much. Saturday, Mom, Jeremy and I went out for dinner and yesterday we were at my grandparents'. You know, the usual weekend stuff. Pretty boring, actually."

The three friends were nearly at school before they caught up with Anne, Monica and Trevor. Alecia was almost glad to see Trevor, although it didn't take long for him to annoy her again.

"So you guys lost on Saturday?" Anne began, slipping her arm through Alecia's. "Too bad."

"I don't even want to talk about it," moaned Alecia.

"I heard about that game," Trevor said. "You might need a tighter defence next time. Don't give them any room to move." When no one said anything, he continued. "We had a tough game too, against the Dynamos. Man! They're nasty. Our centre got cut across his thigh, and needed five stitches. But I scored twice, once off a header. I was — Oh! There's the bell. See ya."

"What an ego!" Anne cried, as Trevor disappeared inside the school.

"I'll say." Alecia and Laurie chimed in unison.

"He knows a lot about soccer," Monica said, in Trevor's defence. "He's the best player on the Mavericks, don't forget."

"Yeah, second-worst team in the league," Laurie snorted. "I don't care if he's the star player — he doesn't have the right to coach us without even watching the game."

"Even if he had watched the game," Alecia muttered.

"I'm just saying ..."

"Don't try to defend Trevor Lunden to me or Laurie, Monica, because it won't work. Just because you think he's Mr. Wonderful doesn't mean we do."

Monica opened her mouth to say more but caught Alecia's eye. In a huff, she flipped her dark hair over her shoulder and kept quiet as they headed inside.

4

False Accusations

W e're going to work on some aerial control drills tonight, ladies," Jeremy announced at practice Tuesday night. "We start by getting into partners."

Alecia paired off with Nancy. A few seconds later, Allison and Rianne came up beside them. Alecia tossed the ball over-hand to Nancy, who trapped it with her chest, let it hit the ground, then kicked it back to Alecia.

"I hate this drill," Nancy muttered.

She leapt in the air for Alecia's overhand shot, but couldn't reach it. The ball rolled across the floor. Nancy ran after it and took her time returning.

"Did you hear that someone from the team got caught shoplifting?" Allison asked. She trapped the ball and sent it back to Rianne.

"You're kidding! Who?" Nancy asked.

"You're not going to believe it," Allison lowered her voice and looked around. "Marnie!"

Alecia caught the ball and stared at Allison.

"No way," she said, shaking her head. "I don't believe Marnie would do anything like that. You must have heard wrong."

"You should be careful, Allison," Alecia warned.

"Oh, don't play 'Coach's Daughter' on us, Alecia!" Rianne cried, bouncing the ball.

"I heard that whoever it is got grounded forever. My parents would freak if I got caught doing something like that," Allison continued.

"Mine too," Nancy agreed.

Alecia caught sight of Jeremy moving in their direction and cleared her throat. "I think we should practice and not talk so much," she said.

* * *

Saturday morning Alecia was tying her cleats before their game against the Tornadoes, when Allison and Rianne came and sat down beside her.

"So did you hear anymore about that shoplifting thing?" Rianne asked as they opened their bags.

Alecia stiffened, but kept her head down as Allison answered in a stage whisper.

"Actually I did! I heard Marnie was working with someone else. It was all planned — just like a movie heist."

"Where did you hear that?"

"Oh, it's all over my school! I guess it happened near there or something. And I'm pretty sure Lexi was with her. The second girl was wearing that sweatshirt Lexi always has on — the black one with the purple lightning marks. I can see Lexi acting as the foil — she'd get into some argument with the clerk ..."

Alecia stood up and walked away. She wished Allison and Rianne wouldn't keep talking about it. They were throwing around gossip like it was fact. What if they were wrong? Thankfully the ref blew the whistle, and Alecia put Allison's words out of her mind as she jogged across the field to her position.

Rain poured down as the game began and within minutes Alecia and her teammates were soaked. Her hair came loose from its braid and got in her eyes, making it difficult to see.

Laurie won the toss and kicked the ball to Lexi. She returned it to Laurie, who turned and headed back toward her own end. The Tornadoes scrambled in confusion, trying to get back over the centre line. But Laurie had already turned again and was charging straight up the middle toward the Tornadoes' goal. The keeper moved out of her net, making herself larger. She bounced on the balls of her feet, and had her gloved hands up in front of her.

Just as Laurie got set to kick, a defender slid into her, knocking the ball just far enough that a teammate got it and sent it flying up the field.

Alecia kicked it away from the Tornado winger and dribbled it back down the field. A large defender challenged her for the ball. Alecia kept control long enough to pass it to Lexi.

Lexi trapped the pass and darted through several Tornado players, getting closer and closer to their net. Waiting right up close to the goal, Allison waved her arms.

"Pa-a-a-a-ss!" she shrieked.

But Lexi didn't seem to hear her. Alecia stayed in close, ready to take a pass if Lexi tried one, but Lexi had her head down and looked only at the ball.

"I'm open, Lex!" Allison yelled.

"Pass to Allison!" Laurie called from the middle of the field, but Lexi kept charging toward the net. At the last second she stopped, sidestepped a charging defender, then took the shot from a bad angle. The ball went wide and the goalkeeper caught it.

"What was that, Lexi?" Allison cried as they prepared for the throw in. Lexi ignored her.

A Tornado winger caught the throw in with her chest, steadied the ball with her foot and then charged up the field as though she was on fire. Nancy and Alecia were hot on her heels.

The winger still in possession of the ball reached the other end of the field but made a sloppy pass when Nancy challenged her. The Tornadoes' forward gained control of the ball and carried it deep into the Burrards' end. She passed off to their centre who was waiting at the net. Suddenly the ball was behind Karen.

The Burrards groaned. Several dirty looks were thrown in Lexi's direction.

"What was that, Lexi?" Allison cried as soon as the ref blew the whistle for half time. "Why didn't you pass? I was open. I could have scored!"

"Yeah, Lexi! You cost us a goal! We are supposed to be a team. We work together, remember?" Rianne added.

"A team? Is that what this is?" Lexi's face was dark with anger. "I'm sorry, I couldn't tell, with all the backstabbing and gossip flying around!"

Alecia groaned. Lexi had overheard Rianne and Allison!

"What are you talking about, Lexi?" Laurie asked as she joined the group. "What rumours?"

"These two," Lexi pointed at Allison and Rianne, "think I planned some kind of shoplifting job with Marnie! I heard them before the game started."

Several of the girls started muttering and casting surprised looks at both Marnie and Lexi. Marnie went beet red, and Alecia thought she saw tears in her eyes. Lexi was just angry — her hands clenched in tight fists at her sides.

"I didn't want anyone to know!" Marnie cried suddenly.

"So it's true then?" someone asked and the muttering began again.

"Marnie was *accused* of shoplifting," Laurie explained. "But she's innocent and has been cleared. She didn't want anyone to know because she's embarrassed — even though she's not guilty. Now, because of this stupid gossiping, she's had to admit to something she wanted to keep quiet. Lexi has been wrongly accused too."

"Is that true girls?" Jeremy asked, joining the group, his face stern.

Allison and Rianne squirmed, but Allison finally nodded. "I'm sorry, Marn, and Lexi. I didn't mean for things to get out of control."

Jeremy ran a hand through his sandy hair and sighed. "You girls should know better than to spread rumours. We have to stick together as a team, and stand up for each other. Now go and get something to drink. We still have twenty minutes left to play and we're down by a goal."

The girls drifted away in small groups. Every so often, they glanced toward Lexi and Marnie. A bad feeling still hung over the Burrards' bench. Alecia couldn't wait for the game to end so she could go home.

5

Commitment

It was pretty bad. Lexi was yelling at Allison and Rianne, and poor Marnie looked close to tears," Alecia told Anne on Monday morning as they walked to school. "I've never seen Laurie so mad before."

"Did Lexi calm down?"

"Yeah — finally. She's not speaking to Allison but at least she finished the game. Marnie's a great team player. She played hard the second half, stopping a bunch of shots. Not that it mattered — we lost anyway."

"Poor Marnie! She must have been embarrassed. And Lexi too."

"How was your weekend?" Alecia was tired of thinking about the problems with the Burrards. It made her head ache. "Did you see Tyler?" Anne's eyes shone as she nodded. Alecia grinned, glad to see her friend so happy. "That's so great, Anne. He's a nice guy. Does your mom know about him yet?"

Anne sighed as she shook her head and the light went out of her eyes. "I hate keeping things from her, but I'm afraid if I tell her she might tell Dad. And he'll blow a fuse if he finds out. It's so silly. Look, Connor and Trevor are waiting for us."

"Connor, I have to ask you something." Anne pulled him aside and left Alecia to walk with Trevor.

They walked in awkward silence. She was ready for him to attack her soccer team or insult girls in general like he usually did, but Trevor was quiet, and seemed preoccupied.

"Did you play this weekend?" he asked at last.

"Yeah, we lost 1–0."

"That's tough. When is your big tournament?"

"Next month."

They didn't look at each other if they could help it. Alecia snuck quick glances at him a couple of times. Monica was always going on about how cute Trevor was — his hazel eyes behind the wire-rimmed glasses that always slipped down his nose, and sandy blond hair that stuck up at odd angles. Maybe she's right, Alecia thought — looking at the spattering of freckles across his cheeks. She blushed and stared at the ground.

"So Connor says you're an only child," Trevor said finally.

"Yeah. How 'bout you?"

"Yeah. Well, technically anyway. My stepdad has two kids from his last marriage, but they live with their mom in Delta."

It was strange how many things she had in common with Trevor — strange and unsettling. She could feel him looking at her, and stared harder at the sidewalk.

"You have a stepfather, too, don't you?"

"I did, yeah. Jeremy and Mom got married a while ago, but he adopted me last month."

Why was she saying so much? This was none of Trevor's business! Her mouth seemed to have a mind of its own.

"Where's your real dad?"

Alecia bristled a bit at the "real" part — Jeremy was her real dad — but she answered politely. "He died when I was four. He had cancer."

"Oh, I'm sorry."

"I don't remember him very well. My Mom met Jeremy when I was six, so he's the only dad I've really ever known. Do you see your dad?"

"Yeah, he lives in North Vancouver," Trevor shrugged. "He's a stockbroker. He's got a massive house with a pool and tennis court. He's always having parties for clients."

Alecia looked up and met Trevor's eye. Something in his tone made her guess that things weren't great between them, despite all the cool stuff. Trevor blinked and looked away. After that, he changed the subject.

"I saw a good soccer movie about some girls who play in England. Have you seen it?"

"I don't think so — what's it called?"

"I can't remember," Trevor replied. He kicked the pavement in frustration. "They were good players too. One scene reminded me of a game we had last month. We were down two goals, and our coach put me in. I was so hot that day! A one-man wrecking crew! The best —"

"Why do you do that?" Alecia stopped in front of the school, glaring at Trevor.

"Do what?" Trevor asked, shaking his head.

"Brag so much about how wonderful you are!"

"I don't."

Alecia looked disgusted. Had they really just finished having a perfectly nice conversation? And had she really thought he was cute a couple of seconds ago? Maybe if he never opened his mouth …

"What are you guys talking about?" Connor jumped in front of them, and Anne was just behind him on the path.

"Nothing. I better go. I've got a test first thing. See ya!" Trevor said, and he disappeared inside the school.

"You look ticked, Alecia," Connor said.

"Yeah, Leesh, what's wrong?" Anne asked. "Did Trevor say something?"

"Your buddy, Connor, is always bragging about what a great soccer player he is! It drives me crazy."

"He doesn't mean anything, Leesh. He just doesn't know how to talk to girls. He's shy."

Alecia had to laugh. "Shy — right! Egotistical is more like it," she said hotly.

Connor suppressed a smile, then glanced at his watch. "I've got that same test!" he said, scrambling to keep up with Trevor.

The two girls went inside and by the time they got to their lockers, Alecia's anger had subsided. She spun the lock on her locker door.

"Good morning!" Monica appeared as Alecia gathered her books. "Guess what!" she cried excitedly. It's so amazing!"

"Monica, what are you talking about?"

Monica grinned broadly. "We're going to Disneyland! Mom and Dad meant it to be a surprise, but Cameron found the tickets by accident so they had to tell us. We leave on Saturday! We're going for two weeks, so we'll get to see a lot of California too."

"That's wonderful, Monica." Anne clapped her hands together.

"Mom and Dad found a package deal. I want to go on every ride. I'll send you guys a postcard — promise!"

* * *

Lexi was in a terrible mood at Tuesday night's practice. "Move your stuff, Alecia," she snapped as she approached the crowded bench.

"Find somewhere else to sit," said Alecia. "There isn't room here."

Lexi dropped her bag on the bench anyway.

"Cut it out, Lexi," Alecia cried as her own bag and water bottle slid to the floor.

"Girls, that's enough. Lexi, if there's not enough room, find somewhere else to put your things," Jeremy said.

"I should have known you'd take your daughter's side," Lexi complained.

"Lexi ..." Jeremy warned.

Lexi grabbed her bag and stormed off to a corner, muttering under her breath. Alecia picked her things up off the floor and put them back on the bench.

Lexi wasn't the only one still upset by what happened last Saturday. Throughout practice little fights kept erupting. Tempers were short and motives were questioned. By halfway, several girls weren't even trying to follow the drills. Lexi wasn't speaking to Rianne or Allison, Marnie was near tears the whole night, and Laurie spent the entire time trying to smooth ruffled feathers. Back in the car with Jeremy, Alecia was completely discouraged.

"You're very quiet, Leesh," Jeremy pointed out gently.

"It seems like there's been one thing after another with this team." Alecia turned to face her father in the dark car. "Half the girls aren't even trying — plus there's all that gossip stuff."

Jeremy sighed and turned on the wipers as rain spattered the windshield. "I don't know what to tell you, Leesh," he said slowly. "You girls are definitely going through some turmoil."

Alecia wasn't surprised that Jeremy had no magic words to offer. What could he say? Only a few weeks ago, the Burrards had been poised to win the championship and now they could barely make it through a practice. Alecia had just begun to realize how much she liked her team, and now it seemed as though there wouldn't be a team for much longer.

"I just hope we make it through the rest of the season in one piece." She fell silent.

Jeremy leaned over and squeezed Alecia's hand. She looked up at him, her eyes troubled.

6

Group Date

Thursday afternoon Alecia was alone at her locker when Trevor appeared. They hadn't seen much of each other since she'd yelled at him on Monday morning.

"Looks like you've got lots of work," Trevor observed.

Alecia balanced her clarinet case on top of her books while she struggled for her coat. "Yeah, I guess —" The clarinet slipped off the books and headed for the floor. Trevor grabbed it just in time, but instead of giving the instrument back to her, he held it.

"How long have you played clarinet?" he asked.

"Oh, a couple of years ..." Alecia slid her jacket on and did up the zipper. She was totally uncomfortable with Trevor standing so close. What did he want?

"Do you like it?"

"It's okay. I don't practise as much as I should. My mom is always nagging me about it." There she went again, talking more than she wanted. She reached for the case again, but Trevor moved out of her way.

"That's all right, I've got it."

"I can carry my own clarinet, Trevor," Alecia said firmly. She thought for a second he was going to pull it away from her again, but Connor arrived and Trevor let go.

"Hey Connor," Alecia said, relieved to see him.

Connor was slouched over and had his hands shoved deep in the pockets of his jacket. His usual bounce was missing. She'd noticed over the last few days that he seemed down, but she hadn't been alone with him to ask why.

"What's going on?" he asked.

"Nothing. Trevor was just helping me with my clarinet."

"Hey! Did Trevor talk to you yet?" Connor asked, brightening. "A whole bunch of us want to get together one night. You have to come, Leesh. Me, Laurie, Tyler, Annie, Trevor and you."

Get together — with *Trevor*? Alecia's heart sank. That would mean listening to his stupid comments all night. She opened her mouth to say 'no,' but then thought of Anne and sighed.

"I guess I can go. I'll have to ask, though."

"That's great! Annie'll be thrilled."

Alecia glanced at Trevor, who was picking his ear, and then looked away. She hoped Anne appreciated her sacrifice.

* * *

"Where's Mom?" Alecia asked, entering the kitchen Friday evening. Jeremy sat at the table by himself, eating a bowl of leftover chili. The newspaper lay spread out in front of him.

"She had a meeting, remember?" He looked up briefly, then went back to the paper.

"Oh, yeah. I forgot."

Alecia rifled through the cupboard looking for a bowl. The chili container was still half full, so she put a bowlful in the microwave. She leaned against the counter, waiting for the food to heat.

The microwave beeped. Alecia carried her meal to the table and slid into a chair beside Jeremy. As usual, she'd overheated the food and burned her tongue on the first bite. Frantically, she reached for Jeremy's water and drained what little was left in the glass.

"That's not water …" he warned. "Sorry. If I'd known you were going to steal my glass I would have warned you ahead of time. Are you okay?"

Alecia could hear Jeremy's laughter and she glared at him. "No, thanks to you," she said, coughing.

"Hey, I wasn't the one who overheated her food — again! Haven't you ever heard the saying 'less is more'?"

I like my food hot. I just have to remember to blow on it first."

They grinned at each other and finished their dinner in silence.

"What's happening now?" Alecia asked, licking the last spoonful of chili.

"What do you mean, what's happening?"

"Exactly what I said. Weren't we going to a movie, or play video games, or something?" Alecia got up and took their dishes to the counter. "Want dessert? I think there's still some of Grandma's apple pie."

"Yes please, and don't be stingy with the ice cream." Jeremy folded the paper and tossed it on to the pile by the back door. He leaned back in his chair and folded his hands behind his head. "So I have to entertain you, do I?"

"You used to do it all the time. I loved it when you came over to see Mom, because you either brought me something or took me somewhere. What happened to that guy?"

"Haven't we had this conversation before? It's like I tell your mother all the time — now that I've won you, I don't have to try anymore. Isn't that the way it works?"

Alecia put two plates down on the table, then reached over and smacked Jeremy on the arm. "That's the biggest load of —"

"Watch it," Jeremy warned, waving a fork at her.

"I think we should rent a movie that Mom would hate, and time it so that the worst part comes on just when she gets home," Alecia suggested.

"Then maybe she'll make a face and say, "You two can watch this nonsense if you want but I'm going up to bed," Jeremy said, mimicking Alecia's mom almost perfectly.

Alecia laughed and a piece of apple flew from her mouth. She covered her mouth with her hand, trying to control the giggling until she could swallow. "Then she'll make that little 'humph' sound and flounce up the stairs."

"Flounce. Now there's a good word," Jeremy said. "So what movie do we get?"

* * *

On Saturday night Laurie's mom picked up Alecia and Anne at Alecia's house and drove the girls to the movie theatre. Laurie promised that they would be right there waiting when she came back to get them.

"Does she always give so many warnings, Laurie?" Alecia whispered as they made their way to the doors.

"Yes. It's so annoying!"

The boys were waiting for them, and the six friends headed inside together. The air was filled with the buttery smell of popcorn, warm bodies and the syrupy scent of pop. Huge screens in the lobby announced the latest movie releases, while the sound of crashing cars and gunfights mingled with the raised voices of people waiting in line. Alecia and her friends bought their tickets,

then stood in another line for snacks before they made their way
to the theatre.

Alecia balanced her drink and box of popcorn as they
hunted for six seats together. The theatre was filling and the
friends discovered that six together wasn't going to work.

"Well, here are four seats," Connor nudged Laurie along the
aisle. "Quick, grab them!"

Within seconds, Trevor and Alecia found themselves in the
aisle alone. Alecia glared at Connor. Anne gave her a sympa-
thetic glance, but Trevor had already found two seats behind
them and was motioning to Alecia to follow him.

"Is this okay?" he asked as Alecia squeezed past half a
dozen people before she reached the seat.

She nodded as she put her drink in the holder and tucked her
popcorn between her knees. She wanted to pelt popcorn at Connor's head, but stuffed it in her mouth instead.

"I hope this movie is good. The last one I saw with this actor
was excellent."

"Oh, yeah! Was that the one with the police detective who
took the drug money or something? Anne is great at remembering movie plots, aren't you Annie?" Once again, Alecia's nerves
made her talk excitedly, but silence wasn't much better.

"Go ahead — try me!" Anne said, turning in her seat. "If I
saw it, I can tell you about it. But don't ask me Alecia's phone
number. I can't remember numbers."

"That's funny. I remember everyone's phone numbers and
birthdays, not plots of books or movies. Isn't that weird?" Alecia felt like a babbling idiot.

Anne faced the front again as Tyler spoke to her. Alecia
shoved another handful of popcorn in her mouth and glanced at
her watch.

"I can rhyme off hockey statistics but not multiplication

facts," Trevor said, pushing his glasses up his nose.

"Hockey stats? I don't get hockey," Alecia said. "My dad watches Hockey Night in Canada every Saturday night, though. And he keeps close track of the Canucks."

"I love hockey but I can't skate. That's why I play soccer. Someday, though, I might like to be a hockey commentator. They're so smart; can you imagine how much hockey stuff they have in their brains? That's what I want to do when I finish school."

He caught her eye and they smiled at each other. Then Trevor looked down at his popcorn and Alecia grabbed her drink from the holder.

7

Conversations

I was wondering," Alecia began Sunday morning at breakfast, "if it would be okay for me to go out next weekend. Apparently it was so successful last night they want to do it again."

She looked up and met her mother's eye across the table. Her mom raised one eyebrow at the sarcastic tone in Alecia's voice but answered evenly.

"That sounds fine, Leesh." Mrs. Parker drained her coffee cup and rose from the table. "Dad or I could drive one way."

"Great. Thanks."

"It seems like yesterday all you kids were fighting in the sandbox," Jeremy said, standing, "and now Annie has a boyfriend."

He picked up the newspaper and headed into the living room.

"Anne has a boyfriend?" Mrs. Parker asked. Is that who I saw her with at your last soccer game?"

"Yes — Tyler," Alecia said slowly.

"That's hard to believe. Anne has always been so shy. I'm surprised that Mr. Leung is allowing her to date, actually. He always seemed so strict.

"Maybe he changed his mind," Alecia muttered.

She stacked the dirty plates and carried them to the counter.

Her mother rinsed each dish carefully, and Alecia put them in the dishwasher.

"What do you think of your friends having boyfriends?" her mom asked casually.

"I don't care. It's their decision."

Alarm bells rang in Alecia's head. She'd never been comfortable talking about boys with her mother. Whenever the topic had come up in the past she had changed the subject, but her mom seemed intent on it now. Alecia poured soap in the dispenser and closed the dishwasher door. She edged toward the hall.

"I remember when all my friends starting going out with boys, and no one was asking me," her mother pressed. "I felt left out."

"Well, I don't."

"Come and sit with me for a few minutes." Alecia's mom pulled out a chair from the table.

"Mom …"

"You can't keep running from this subject forever. Your friends are exploring these relationships and I want to know how you feel about it. I got a sense that you weren't thrilled with how things went last night. Did you want to talk about what happened?"

Wasn't it obvious to her mother that Alecia *didn't* want to talk about it?

"I don't 'feel' anything about it! I don't have a boyfriend. I don't like a boy. I don't need a sex talk!"

Her mom rested her chin on her clasped hands and gazed at Alecia. "You may not like a particular boy right now, Leesh, but down the road …"

"We can talk about it then," Alecia said. She picked at her nails, avoiding her mother's eyes.

"I like the way you and your friends are going out in a group together. That's a good idea."

"Except that I keep getting paired off with Trevor."

"Is that bad?"

"He's a jerk. He's always bragging about how great he is at soccer and telling Laurie and I how to play."

Her mother smiled. "What?" Alecia snapped.

"He's just not sure how to be with girls, Leesh. He's trying to impress you with his knowledge of soccer. Don't let it bother you."

Alecia pulled at a paper serviette left on the table. She rolled tiny pieces in her fingers and made a little pile. Why would Trevor Lunden want to impress her?

"Whatever. He's still an idiot. Anyway, I'm supposed to meet Connor right now." She jumped to her feet. "Can I go?"

Mrs. Parker sighed and sat back in her chair. "Yes, go," she said but Alecia was already gone.

* * *

Alecia met Connor at the elementary school playground and they sat on the swings. Soon she was soaring through the air, the wind blowing her long blonde hair behind, then whipping it into her face. Connor sat in his swing, kicking at the sand with his shoe. He grabbed an apple from his pocket. After a few minutes Alecia let her swing slowly come to a stop.

"It feels like we haven't seen each other for months," said Alecia.

"I know what you mean," Connor nodded.

"I miss it, you know? I liked it when you, me and Annie did stuff together. Now everybody else is around all the time."

"You don't like Trevor much, do you Leesh?" Connor threw

bits of his apple to the crows at his feet.

"No," said Alecia firmly. "He always says such stupid things! And he's so stuck on himself."

"I keep warning him about that but he doesn't get it."

"Yeah, well, it's annoying. And now we all have to go out together. I know it's to help Anne and Tyler, but I always get stuck with Trevor, and I don't like it. Why can't the four of you go by yourselves?"

Connor threw his apple core at the greedy crows and wiped his hands on his jeans. Finally he looked at Alecia.

"Laurie and I —" He stopped talking and stared at the ground. Alecia's heartbeat quickened as she waited for him to continue. "We've been fighting a lot lately. The only time we see each other is when we go out with the rest of you. So you're kind of helping us, too."

Alecia looked surprised. "What's wrong, Connor? You guys are so good together."

He brushed again at his jeans, although there was nothing on them. "Laurie's busy, I guess — with soccer and music lessons and her friends. She says I'm lazy, and that I never want to do stuff."

Connor looked so sad, Alecia felt badly for him, and for Laurie too. "What are you going to do?"

Connor shrugged and stood up. "My mom says we're only fourteen, and that we're too young to be serious about one person. Maybe she's right."

Alecia got to her feet and stood awkwardly for a second. Then she reached out and gave Connor a quick hug. He stiffened a bit at her touch but when she pulled away, he was smiling at her. "Thanks, Leesh. I should have talked to you about it sooner, but —"

"You like each other a lot. Maybe you'll find a way of making

it work," said Alecia positively. You are kind of lazy, by the way,"
she teased.

But Connor didn't laugh or tease her back. He just looked
miserable. "Laurie liked that about me before. She said I made
her slow down a bit. Now she seems bored. Plus, I think she
likes this guy in her math class, Evan or Ethan somebody. She's
always going on about "Ethan this" or "Ethan that." I saw them
talking in the hall the other day, and when I came up they
stopped. Laurie looked totally embarassed."

Alecia felt badly for her friend, but she had never been very
good at saying the right thing in times like these, so she kept
quiet and just squeezed Connor's elbow.

8

Struggling

Tuesday night Jeremy worked at various drills with Karen and their new backup goalkeeper. Alecia thought it looked like a firing squad — Karen standing in net while they all took shots at her. In between kicks, Karen fidgeted nervously at the ball.

Alecia sighed as yet another shot went behind Karen into the net. Since their loss against the Wolverines, Karen's confidence seemed to be slipping away. Jeremy had talked to her, and worked with her every practice, but he just couldn't get their goalkeeper to relax and focus.

"For crying out loud, Karen!" Lexi kicked at a stray ball. "Catch the balls!"

"Lexi, Karen's trying," Jeremy called.

"No, she's not. She's afraid of the ball. You can't be a good goalkeeper if you're afraid of the ball, Karen."

"Well, we wouldn't need a new goalkeeper if you hadn't chased Stacie off," Rianne said under her breath.

Luckily Alecia was the only one who heard her. She hooked her hand under Rianne's elbow and pulled her off to the side away from the team.

Rianne scowled. "Lexi's so negative all the time!" she said to Alecia. "She corrects everyone, even though Jeremy and

Laurie tell her not to, and she never says anything nice about anyone. Look at poor Karen — what a mess!"

"You're right, she is. And Lexi doesn't help. But blaming Lexi for Stacie leaving does no good and what we really need is to help Karen, right? Maybe if you and I encourage her we might block out some of Lexi's criticism," suggested Alecia.

"I don't know," Rianne sighed. "What good are the two of us going to be?"

"Better than nothing, don't you think?"

Reluctantly Rianne agreed and the two girls went back to the practice. From then on, every time Karen made a block or redirected the ball Rianne and Alecia praised her. And if she mishandled the ball they shouted out "good effort," drowning out any of Lexi's comments. After a while, the other girls joined in and by the end of the night Karen was smiling.

On the way home Jeremy reached over and squeezed Alecia's knee. "I was pleased to see the way you took control at practice tonight, Leesh. You and Rianne helped to improve Karen's confidence."

"Thanks ..."

"Seriously," Jeremy insisted. "You saw a bad situation, addressed the problem and came up with a solution. Part of being a team leader is taking initiative and that's what you did tonight. I'm proud of you."

"Thanks Jer — Dad." The word "Dad" felt awkward on her tongue but she was glad she'd finally tried it. And really, it wasn't so bad after all.

Jeremy turned to look at her, a smile stretching across his face. He opened his mouth, then closed it again and turned back to the road. "That has a nice ring to it." There was a catch in his voice.

"Well, I'll probably still call you Jeremy half the time anyway ..."

* * *

"Did you hear from Laurie?" Alecia asked her father as they walked to the field Sunday morning. "I didn't see her at school Friday."

"She called." Jeremy set the bag of practice balls down on the frozen ground. "She still sounds rough but said she'd try to be here."

"We really need her."

Across the field the Burrards' archrivals, the Rocketeers, were gathered around their coach. This was the last time the two teams would play each other before the finals. Alecia scanned the girls and stopped, her eyes widening.

"Hey, look — it's Stacie!"

She pointed across the field to Stacie Hutchins leaning against the opposing goalpost.

"So it is. Well, I don't know why she wouldn't join another team, she's a good goalkeeper."

Alecia stared at him. "But the Rocketeers? They have a good goalkeeper."

"Actually, I remember hearing that her family moved away."

One by one, the Burrards straggled on to the field. Alecia spotted Laurie and ran over to her. "Are you playing?" she cried, but her smile faded as she caught sight of Laurie's puffy eyes and red nose.

"I want to —" Laurie was overcome by a sudden fit of coughing. Her eyes watered and the effort left her totally weak.

Alecia shook her head. "You can't play, you can barely breathe!"

"I felt better when I woke up. There is no way I'm missing this game," replied Laurie. "Our record is slipping and the district finals are only a few weeks away!" she added, sinking to the bench.

"Well, we'll have to win without you. You can't play."

Before Laurie could answer Allison came running up. "Stacie's playing for the Rocketeers! Can you believe it?" she cried.

Laurie looked across the field and her shoulders slumped as she spotted their former goalkeeper. Then she straightened. "Don't panic. Yes, she's a great goalkeeper and hard to score against, but we know her tricks."

"Laurie's right," Allison agreed. "We also know her weak spots. This could be a good thing!"

"Okay, girls, you're on!" Jeremy called ending the conversation.

* * *

At halftime, the score was tied 1–1. The Rocketeers' centre drove the ball hard up the centre. Marnie challenged for possession. Alecia shadowed them by staying close, ready to pick up the ball if Marnie kicked it away. She was covered with bruises and got a nasty cut on her shin from trying to intercept a pass. The angle of the sun made it difficult to see.

"Go hard!" someone cried from the bench.

"Come on Burrards!"

Marnie checked the opposing centre and picked up the ball. She found Alecia open and chipped the ball to her. Alecia settled the pass and headed upfield.

Stacie was causing big trouble for the Burrards. Alecia had always been in awe of the way she threw herself around the net with no concern for her own safety. But it had always been in their favour before. Now the situation had changed.

Alecia passed off to Lexi, who was tackled by a Rocketeer defender and sent sprawling to the ground.

The whistle blew and Lexi was awarded a free kick. Murmurings went up around the field as everyone took their positions. A showdown! Alecia's heart raced. All morning Stacie had been making comments whenever the play was near her net. Lexi had to beat her!

Lexi took a deep breath and rolled her head from side to side, loosening her muscles. Stacie stood out of her net — knees bent, hands up, eyes glinting with concentration. Her turquoise and purple jersey was blinding in the brilliant sunlight.

Lexi took one last breath and began to run. She gained speed as she approached Stacie, dribbling skillfully. At the last second she feinted left and let go with a powerhouse kick that headed for Stacie's left shoulder. The ball soared through the sky, looking like it was going to sail right over Stacie as she struggled to recover from the fake left. But when Stacie landed on the ground, she cradled the ball safely in her arms.

The Rocketeers cheered. Stacie kicked the ball back onto the field and play resumed. A Rocketeer forward trapped the ball with her chest and raced toward the goal. Her shot caught Karen off guard and suddenly the score was 2–1.

At the end of the game the two teams lined up to shake hands. Alecia joined the line behind Karen. The continuous chant of "Good game," "Good game," ran through her head. It hadn't felt like a good game. It stank, actually. Alecia barely noticed shaking hands as she puzzled over the Burrards' less than sparkling performance.

"Still happy with your choice?" Stacie asked, pulling Alecia back to the field.

"We didn't make a choice, Stacie, you did," Alecia told her. "You didn't want to play with Lexi so you quit."

"I always held the Burrards together, Alecia. Don't you know that?"

Alecia struggled to think of something to say that would put Stacie Hutchins in her place but nothing came. In another second Stacie went off laughing, leaving Alecia standing by herself.

9

What Do We Do Now?

"Did she really say that?" Laurie asked under her breath.

Alecia nodded and glanced over at Jeremy, who was working on a drill with several players. She hadn't said anything to him, or anyone else about Stacie's comment.

"I couldn't believe it. I mean, we all know Stacie has a big ego, but 'held this team together'?"

Laurie shrugged. "If you think about it, Leesh, aren't we proving her right? We haven't been playing well since she left."

Alecia sighed and rubbed at her temples. The district finals were coming up soon, and the way things were going the Burrards would get eliminated in the first round.

"We have to do something, Alecia. We have to tell everybody what Stacie said to you — get them to try harder. I want that title! We deserved it a month ago."

The two girls looked at each other in silence. Then Alecia had a thought.

"What if we talk to everybody separately?"

"You mean, tell them what Stacie said?" Laurie asked.

Alecia smiled slowly as the idea took shape. "We could make up a script, so that we say the same thing," she said. "What if we suggest that it's best if we just fold the team?"

"Fold the team?" Laurie parroted. "I don't want to fold the —

oh, I get it! Reverse psychology, right?"

"Right!" Alecia nodded. "Tell them one thing to get them to do another. My mother always tries it on me."

"Do you fall for it?" Laurie asked, a note of worry creeping into her voice.

Alecia blushed. "Yeah, sometimes …"

Laurie laughed but then a shadow fell across her face. "What if everyone wants to quit?"

"We don't have much of a team right now anyway, do we? But I don't think they will want to give up. It's worth a try."

"You're right. I don't want to see the Burrards disbanded, but I want to play soccer. I'm not a very good captain, am I?"

"Laurie, don't beat yourself up about this. It's no one's fault." Finally Laurie straightened.

"I never thought things would get this bad, did you?" she asked.

"No. And I never thought I'd be fighting so hard for this team."

At the end of practice Laurie and Alecia huddled together again to go over their plan. When they were finished Alecia cleared her throat.

"Listen, Laurie, it's none of my business, but I was talking to Connor the other day —"

"He told you we're fighting, right?"

"Well, yeah. He said things weren't great between you."

"Well, they're not, Leesh. I don't think we're going to stay together."

Something in Laurie's voice was different — something hard and almost unpleasant. Alecia hesitated before she spoke again.

"Can't you work it out? I mean, Connor is really unhappy."

"I'm unhappy too, Alecia. It's hard being with someone

who never wants to do anything ... but I don't really want to talk about it. You're Connor's friend and my teammate and it isn't fair to put you in the middle."

Alecia felt as though she'd been slapped but she nodded and went to wait for her dad in the car.

* * *

On Wednesday morning Alecia walked to school with Connor. He was quiet and Alecia, busy with her own thoughts, didn't try to break the silence. When they reached the school, Connor stopped her.

"Laurie told me you tried to talk to her," he said.

Alecia blushed, waiting for a lecture, but instead Connor smiled at her.

"Thanks for the help, Leesh. It means a lot."

"You're welcome, Connor. I hope —" Alecia paused and Connor nodded.

"Me too."

He pulled open the door and they went inside together.

Before they reached their lockers, Alecia heard Monica's voice.

"It was the *best!*" Monica grinned when she spotted Connor and Alecia. "Everyone should definitely go to California. I loved Disneyland and Knott's and California Adventure and Universal Studios! The rides were so amazing! Oh! And I met the cutest guy on Thunder Mountain. He was from Wisconsin and had the coolest accent! But of course he kept telling me I had a cool accent —"

"Did you bring me anything?" Connor interrupted.

"Of course! I brought everyone something!" Monica laughed at everyone's surprised expressions. "Did you think I would for-get all about my friends?"

"You didn't need to buy us anything," Alecia said, rummaging through her locker.

"Oh, I'm not even speaking to you, Ms. Parker!" Alecia shot bolt upright and Monica punched her playfully in the arm. "I go away for two weeks and you steal Trevor away from me!"

"I didn't steal anyone." Alecia rubbed her arm and turned her head to hide the red that was creeping up her neck.

"That's not what I heard!" Monica's voice rang through the hallway. "I heard you guys have gone out a few times — but never mind that. I've got more news! I've decided to have a party for my birthday! Cripes, can you believe I'm going to be fourteen? We're getting so *old*. Of course you're all invited!"

Alecia smiled and nodded with the others but her thoughts drifted away. Maybe now that Monica was back she could be Trevor's "date" and Alecia wouldn't have to listen to him brag.

10

A Few Good Girls

That night Alecia sat on her bed and stared at the "script" she and Laurie had written. She had almost memorized it but still couldn't bring herself to pick up the phone. What if their plan didn't work? Alecia curled the edge of the paper. She didn't want to play for another team.

Her dad stopped at the bedroom door and leaned against the jamb.

"You look very serious. Is everything all right?"

"Just thinking about the Burrards. Laurie and I were talking about the problems. We think we've got a way to fix them, but ..."

"But you aren't ready to discuss it yet. I understand."

"Dad?"

"Yes?"

"Do you regret taking on the Burrards?"

"Not for a minute. We're a good team, Leesh. We aren't winning, but we'll figure it out."

When she was sure Jeremy was downstairs, Alecia shut her bedroom door and flopped back on the bed. She picked up the portable phone and pressed the numbers.

"Hi, Marnie, it's Alecia."

"Hey, Leesh, what's up?"

"Well, actually —" She looked over her script one last time and continued. "Laurie and I have been talking to Jeremy and we think it might be best if we fold the team."

"What? You're kidding, right?" Marnie cried in disbelief.

"Well, first we lost Stacie, then there was all that gossip ... plus everyone seems so busy with other things. We know we won't do well at the finals so we figured we'd be better off quitting now and not embarrassing ourselves. Stacie is probably right anyway — we'll never go anywhere without her."

"Stacie said that?" Marnie snorted. "That girl has too much ego. Our problems have nothing to do with her leaving. We're just not working hard enough as a team. Is it final? I mean, is this decision final?" Marnie asked.

"Well, no. But what's the point? We just keep losing."

"There's no way I'm letting Stacie think she's why the Burrards are losing right now. Come on, Alecia. Don't fold the team."

"I'll let you know, Marn." Alecia smiled as she put a little check beside Marnie's name.

Her next call was to Trina. Alecia pressed the numbers slowly. She didn't know Trina very well. But Trina and Stacie had always been good buddies and both were reluctant to play with Lexi. Who knew how she'd respond.

"I'm phoning about soccer," Alecia said when Trina answered. "Laurie and I have been talking to Jeremy and we think it might be best if we fold the team."

"Why?"

"Well, all that gossip and losing Stacie ..." Alecia ran through her lines for the second time, finishing with, "Stacie is probably right anyway — we'll never manage to go anywhere without her." There was a pause and Alecia could hear Trina breathing.

"It's true. We haven't played well without Stacie. She was

the backbone of our team, you know? I always thought she would have made a better captain than Laurie."

"Laurie tries hard, Trina."

"Well, I think it's a good idea. Think it will work right away?"

"We'll have to talk to everyone first. Anyway, I'd better go. I've got other girls to call."

Alecia said good-bye and hung up the phone. Then she put a little x by Trina's name and tried not to feel discouraged.

* * *

Thursday evening the Burrards practised outside again for the first time since the fall. The ground was fairly dry and despite cool temperatures it promised to be an easier practice. Just having the space to run made a huge difference.

However, as Alecia helped her dad carry the mesh bags of practice gear out to the field, she felt a niggling sense of unease. Where was everyone? Laurie, Allison and a few others were stretching, Karen was putting on her cleats at the bench, but many of the girls were absent.

"Did someone cancel practice and forget to tell me?" Jeremy joked.

"Well, we weren't sure if there was practice tonight," Lexi began but Alecia interrupted.

"Oh, here come a couple more. Everyone's just late." She spoke loudly to drown out Lexi. "I guess you forgot to say something at the end of last practice. Or maybe they forgot it was an outdoor practice." Alecia shrugged innocently.

Jeremy studied her a moment, with questioning eyes, but Laurie called his attention away and Alecia breathed a sigh of relief.

Carefully she tied her cleats and adjusted her shin pads, trying to remember the script. Her heart sank as she realized they hadn't phoned the girls back to let them know the outcome. Laurie came and sat beside her, her face troubled.

"I think we've messed up, Leesh."

The two girls looked at each other. Only half the team was on the field. Jeremy was suspicious, despite Alecia's explanation. And how would they keep everyone from blabbing for the next ninety minutes?

"Well, we're a small group for some reason," Jeremy called. "Maybe I didn't make it clear we were practising here tonight. But the rest of us can work on some things. I know you liked the warmth and dryness of the gym but we'll get a better practice outside on a full field."

Jeremy began with a new drill called "follow the leader." After some frowns and even a few confused looks everyone drifted into groups. Karen and Nancy worked together with Alecia starting as leader.

Before they started Nancy grabbed Alecia's arm. "Why didn't Jeremy say anything about us folding?" she asked. "What happened with all the calls? Are we staying together?"

"Yes," said Alecia. "I guess he didn't want to make too much of it or something. I don't know," she hedged, blushing. She glanced at Jeremy and prayed no one would say anything to him.

She led her group around the field, zigging and zagging. The other two dribbled their soccer balls and tried to keep up, laughing as they collided with each other.

"Well?" Alecia whispered to Laurie later in the practice while they waited for the rest of the team to set up a scrimmage. "What do you think?"

"These girls are working hard," Laurie said slowly. "We haven't had as much chatter, that's for sure. But I'm not getting my hopes up. The girls who haven't shown are the ones who thought we should break up the team. We'll have to call them all, Leesh, and warn them to come up with a good excuse for missing tonight." Alecia nodded in agreement as Jeremy blew his whistle to begin.

Maybe things would be okay after all.

11

Backfire

Hey, Jeremy," Lexi called as the girls were packing up at the end of practice. "A bunch of people are coming across the field."

Jeremy and Alecia glanced at the small group of adults making their way toward them. "They're league officials. What do they want, I wonder?" Jeremy said, puzzled.

"Isn't that your dad, Allison?" Nancy asked.

"Yeah, and Lexi's dad."

The group that stood before Jeremy looked serious.

"Good evening," Jeremy said. "What can I do for you?"

"Lexi tells me that you're thinking of disbanding the team because the girls are losing, Jeremy," Lexi's father said, obviously speaking for everyone.

Alecia froze. The stack of orange cones slipped from her hands and landed with a soft thud in the grass. Beside her she heard Laurie's sharp intake of breath. Jeremy looked around, frowning.

"What authority do you have to disband a team mid-season? As far as I'm aware we're the only ones who can do that," a tall, thin man said.

"You're right, Carson …" Jeremy began.

"And what kind of message does it send our young women

when their coach has no faith in them? They've been playing better this season than other years. In fact, several of us have commented on how happy we are with the coaching change this year," someone else said.

"But now, all of a sudden they're in a slump and you're afraid of being embarrassed?" Allison's father asked, his voice rough.

"I'm sorry," Jeremy said, holding up a hand. "I'm confused. Lexi, who told you the team was being disbanded?"

"Alecia called me the other night. She said you, Laurie and her were thinking of breaking up because we're playing so lousy and you don't want to be embarrassed in the finals."

"Not a great reason to fold, Parker," the man Jeremy had called Carson said. "We've got a lot of angry parents demanding to know what's going on."

"Wait a minute." Jeremy turned to Alecia. "Is that true, Alecia? Did you call Lexi?" Alecia nodded.

"Who else did you call?"

"We called the whole team," Laurie told him.

"So that's why more than half the team is missing tonight …"

"It was my idea, Dad," Alecia admitted. "I convinced Laurie to help me."

Jeremy rubbed a hand through his hair and groaned. "I'm going to have to get to the bottom of this. But I assure you, everyone, I have no intention of disbanding the Burrards. We will play to the end of the season. I apologize for the misunderstanding."

"See that you do. And we'll expect you to talk to the parents."

The group looked as though they had more to say but they only nodded and left. Laurie and Alecia didn't look at each other or their teammates as the rest of the girls slowly gathered their things and headed for the parking lot. Alecia felt sick to her stomach. How had things gone so wrong? Finally Laurie, Alecia and Jeremy were the only ones on the field.

"I'm sorry, Dad ..." Alecia started.

"Yeah, Jeremy. We're sorry ..." Laurie began.

"Let's finish putting these things away. Your mother's waiting for you, Laurie," Jeremy interrupted.

They packed up the car and Laurie — with a last tortured glance at Alecia — went home. Alecia buckled her seat belt and braced herself for trouble.

But Jeremy didn't speak in the car. He drove in silence and when he pulled into the garage, he went straight into the house, leaving Alecia to unload the gear. When she entered the kitchen minutes later, Jeremy was slumped in a chair at the table, eyes closed.

"We shouldn't have used your name, Dad. I'm sorry," Alecia said, standing awkwardly by the door.

"You're right, Alecia, you shouldn't have used my name. But really, you shouldn't have said anything at all. It's not your place to make decisions for the team."

"I just thought if we talked to everyone and got them to see ..."

"And they did see. They saw that their coach and their captain have no faith in them. They saw that when the going gets hard, it's okay to quit. They also saw that winning is the only acceptable outcome."

"No, we wanted everyone to try harder! I didn't know the girls would talk to their parents, or that they'd call the league!"

"Do you have any idea how embarrassing that was tonight, Alecia? Not only was I confronted with angry parents and league officials, but I didn't even know what was going on with my own team. More than half of the girls weren't there, which made it look even worse." Jeremy looked at her, his face creased with disappointment.

"We were just trying to help!" Alecia slammed around the kitchen, trying to escape the look in her father's eyes. "I couldn't stand how badly things were going! Then Stacie said she'd been responsible for holding the team together. I wanted to prove that the Burrards don't need her!" Her voice rose with each sentence until she was yelling. But still her dad answered in a steady voice.

"Why didn't you at least run this by me before you started phoning?"

"I thought you wanted me to take initiative. That's what you said. So I did and now that's wrong too!" If only he would react to her own anger. The sadness in Jeremy's voice, and the disappointed look in his eyes were worse than any yelling would have been.

"I do want you to take initiative and be a leader on the team." He got to his feet, slowly. "But part of that is thinking things through before taking action. Asking advice isn't a sign of weakness, Alecia — it's a sign of strength."

"I was just trying to help!"

"Except that you didn't."

12

Heartbreaker

Alecia was still in her pajamas the next morning, taking advantage of the Professional Day to sleep in and avoid both her parents, when the phone rang.

"I didn't want to call last night. How was it? Is your Dad upset?" Laurie asked.

"He's real disappointed. I wish he'd yelled and thrown things, it would have been better than this." Alecia yawned. She'd tossed and turned, hearing Jeremy's words replaying in her mind all night. "I'll let him cool down, I think. We're going to have to call the girls who didn't go to practice last night and make sure they're at the game Sunday."

"Yeah, I'll tackle my list right now."

"I'm sorry I dragged you into this, Laur."

"I didn't have to go along with it. I'll talk to you later."

Alecia found her team list. She'd just get it over with before she did anything else.

"There's been a mix-up, Trina. Laurie and I forgot to phone you back to tell you the team had decided to keep going. So you should be at the game this weekend, okay?"

"Really? I would have thought more girls would want to fold. Well, I'm not sure if I'm going to play, Leesh. The team hasn't been the same since Stacie left."

"But we need everyone. We only have a couple more weeks, then we're done. If we work hard, I know we can improve."

"I'll think about it, Leesh."

She called Rianne next and was told by her mother that she wasn't home.

"Can you tell her Alecia Parker called from soccer?"

"Is this about the Burrards folding?" Rianne's mother asked. "Because I'm quite prepared to fight ..."

"Oh, no! The Burrards aren't folding. That's why I'm phoning. Rianne wasn't at practice last night and we just wanted to make sure she knows to be at the game this weekend. I'm sorry about what happened. It was my fault and I'm trying to fix it. Can you let Rianne know about the game?"

"I'll tell her."

Alecia called the rest of the girls from her list and spoke to a couple more irate parents. She did her best to apologize, but some of the girls weren't sure about returning and certain parents weren't convinced Jeremy had nothing to do with it. After the last call, she had a headache. She rubbed hard at her temples, trying to ease the pounding. How had her good intentions gone so horribly wrong? And what if this second round of calls hadn't fixed the problem?

She was still sitting by the phone half an hour later when Connor arrived at the back door.

"Laurie broke up with me." Connor slumped down in a chair in the kitchen. His eyes were red and swollen. "She told me last night, right after soccer practice. Supposedly, we've outgrown each other and it's time to move on." Connor wiped his face with the back of his hand and sniffed. "Man, it's a good thing today is a Professional Day or I would have had to skip," he muttered, blowing his nose. "Sorry about this."

"You don't have to apologize." Alecia felt as though her

own heart had been broken. She'd never seen her friend so unhappy. In fact, Connor was the one person in her life she could depend on to pull her out of her own low times.

"I'm the one who's sorry. I know you wanted to make it work," Alecia said.

"Yeah, well, it takes two to do that. Laurie just wanted out. I think she's already going out with that Ethan guy."

"Maybe he'll break up with her and she'll see what it's like," Alecia said with instant regret when she saw Connor's face. "Sorry, I didn't mean that."

"I guess I shouldn't sit here moping." Connor looked up and tried to smile.

"I don't mind. You can mope as long as you want. Are you hungry? I think there's still some Rice Krispie squares here." Alecia got up to look through the cupboards.

She brought the treats to the table along with some milk and glasses. Connor helped himself to a square. He took a bite and chewed noisily, then reached for another one. Alecia caught his eye as he sat back in his chair and smiled.

"I'll be okay, you know," he said. He looked down at the square in his hand and sighed. "Eventually."

* * *

Alecia was reading on the couch later that afternoon when she heard the garage door open. According to the clock above the fireplace it was too early for her mother.

"You're home early ..." She stopped awkwardly when Jeremy entered. They looked at each other, then looked away. They'd said almost nothing to each other since arriving home the night before.

"I have a soccer meeting."

"Is it what I think —"

"No, it's about the finals."

Alecia watched as Jeremy walked through the kitchen and up the stairs to his room. Her eyes stung and her throat burned. Would he ever forgive her? Would their normal teasing and joking ever return? She felt as though a piece of her heart had been torn out.

When Jeremy came downstairs again moments later, Alecia cleared her throat.

"Laurie and I ..."

"Tell your mother I'll be home around seven."

He left before Alecia could answer. She was still staring at the closed door when her mother arrived.

"Where did Jeremy go? I just passed him on the road — Alecia, what's wrong?"

Alecia tried to control the choking sobs erupting from deep inside but they wouldn't be stopped. She collapsed into her mother's arms and cried.

"Is this about last night?" Mrs. Parker asked. Alecia nodded against her mother's chest. "Jeremy's going to get over it, sweetie. Give him time."

"Dad hardly even spoke to me! He probably wishes he'd never adopted me."

Mrs. Parker didn't answer right away. She smoothed Alecia's long hair and rubbed her back. "He might be angry but he doesn't hate you," she said at last. "He was embarrassed by what happened on the field and needs time. Give him another day or so and then speak to him again. Okay?"

Alecia pulled away from her mother and wiped at her damp face. Her nose was running, her eyes were burning and she had the hiccups. "I said I was sorry. Laurie and I tried to fix things today but he didn't want to know. Can't you just talk to him?"

"You and Jeremy have to work this out between you. It isn't my fight, so to speak. Talk to him tomorrow or after your game on Sunday." She leaned over and kissed Alecia's forehead.

Alecia blew her nose and then sat and stared through her bangs at her mother.

13

Damage Control

On Sunday morning Alecia was sitting by herself at the side of the field when a shadow fell across her. She looked up, squinting into the bright light.

"Morning." Laurie sat heavily on the bench beside Alecia. She yawned, covering her mouth with her hand.

"Hi Laurie."

"How's Jeremy?"

"Still upset. We've hardly talked since Thursday, actually."

"Do you think I should say anything?"

"No. My mom says it's best to let Jeremy cool down in his own time. I'm really sorry about all this Laurie."

"I know, Leesh."

They organized their gear quietly. Laurie pulled her shin pads from her bag and stared blankly across the field.

"I guess Connor told you the news?" she asked, turning to Alecia.

"Yeah, he came over Friday." Alecia had been dreading this conversation. "He said you had outgrown each other …"

"The thing is," Laurie began slowly, "I was bored. Connor's not the most active person in the world."

"You knew that all along, though."

"Yeah, but at first he made an effort. Or maybe —" Laurie

stopped, closed her eyes, took a breath and then spoke again slowly. "I know Connor's upset and I'm sorry about that. But I hope we'll still be friends?"

"Sure." Alecia spoke without much conviction. "It's nothing to do with me anyway. We have a game to win, that's all I'm concerned about."

She finished tying her cleats and adjusted her shin pads and socks. When she looked up Laurie was watching her.

"You don't sound okay, Leesh."

"Well, Connor's my best friend and he's upset. You're a teammate and we have to play together, like you said the other day."

"I thought we were friends, too."

"We are, but Connor is the one who got dumped. I didn't think you needed my support — you've already got someone new, right?" The words came out sounding rougher than she'd intended and Alecia realized she was angrier with Laurie than she'd thought. Laurie's eyes filled with tears and she turned away.

"Laurie, wait a second." Alecia grabbed the other girl's arm. "I'm sorry, that wasn't very nice. I didn't mean it the way it came out."

"I'm upset about me and Connor too, Alecia. And just because I'm interested in Ethan doesn't change that. I liked Connor a lot."

"Yeah, I know. Sometimes people just want different things. Listen, it'll be okay. Let's just get through this game and keep our team in one piece. We need to focus on that right now. Okay?"

"Yeah, sure." Laurie zipped her bag shut and walked away.

Alecia sighed in frustration. Being stuck in the middle of this breakup was lousy. Is this what her mother meant about not wanting to get between her and Jeremy's troubles? Alecia's loyalties lay in two places as well. But, like her mother, Alecia had to let Laurie and Connor figure it out themselves.

* * *

"Good win, Burrards," Jeremy told them at the end of the game. "I'll see you all at practice on Tuesday night — our usual time at the *field*. Alecia, Laurie, a word please."

Alecia and Laurie held back while their teammates drifted away in groups of two and three. When they were alone, Jeremy cleared his throat. "Obviously you solved the problem you created. Thanks for taking the initiative. From the looks of things this morning, we may be back on track. I certainly hope so."

"Sorry, Jeremy —"

Jeremy held up a hand, stopping Laurie mid-sentence. "I know you are, Laurie. Let's just go from here, okay?"

Laurie nodded. She swung her bag over her shoulder and headed for the parking lot. Jeremy tucked his whistle and clipboard into his bag. He glanced around one last time, then started to walk away.

"Are you coming?" he called over his shoulder.

"You told Laurie we're okay," Alecia said, still sitting on the bench. "But we're not."

Jeremy turned around and came back. He sat beside Alecia and put his bag down at his feet. "We're not," he repeated.

"No. You hardly even speak to me; you didn't say one word to me during the game … How come you forgive Laurie but not me? I apologized, I tried hard to fix the mistake I made. I don't know what else I'm supposed to do." Tears sprang to her eyes and she blinked rapidly and wiped at her face with her sleeve.

"You're right, I've been holding a grudge. But I was embarrassed, Leesh. And it's hard to just forget and let go."

"You seemed to be able to let go with Laurie." Alecia stared straight ahead, focusing on a distant tree. Jeremy shifted on the bench beside her and his knee bumped Alecia's. She moved her leg over.

Her dad rested his elbows on his knees, hands clasped. He cleared his throat but it was several seconds before he spoke.

"I guess it's harder because you're my daughter. I expect more from you ..."

"But that's not fair!" Alecia swung around to face her dad, stung by the injustice of his words.

"You're right, but that's the way it is." Alecia started to speak but Jeremy stopped her. "I'll try harder to treat you like all the other girls on the team, okay? And I am sorry I was acting so cold."

"I didn't think you loved me anymore," Alecia said softly, most of her anger gone. "That maybe you were sorry you'd adopted me."

Jeremy put his arm around Alecia's shoulders and squeezed her against him. He kissed the top of her head, then rested his chin on her hair. "I could never stop loving you. I've loved you since you were just a gap-toothed little girl with pigtails." Alecia giggled despite herself and Jeremy hugged her tight. "You're my daughter, Alecia. It has nothing to do with a piece of paper, either. It's what you feel. And no matter how badly you mess up or how angry I get, that won't ever change. Okay?"

Alecia nodded. Things didn't seem quite so bleak anymore somehow. "I love you too, Dad."

14

Monica's Party

You have to dance! Come on Annie and Tyler! Dance, everybody! You can't just stand around eating the whole night!" Monica started dragging people into the middle of the room.

Laughing, Tyler and Anne started off and a few others joined them. Alecia sat off to the side watching. Dancing was not her thing. She was too self-conscious.

Monica dragged Trevor out on the floor. Alecia thought she danced with more energy than skill, and tried not to laugh. When the music slowed down, Tyler put his arms around Anne's waist and she hugged his neck. They looked so happy together! Across the room Alecia noticed Connor by himself. He didn't look happy at all.

Life is confusing, thought Alecia. Maybe it was better to be by herself, just hang out with her friends and not worry about boys. She got off the couch and headed for the kitchen.

Alecia was munching on a taco chip when Trevor appeared. He was flushed from dancing with Monica and his glasses had slipped down his nose. Alecia swallowed then managed a faint hello. Her pulse quickened and the jittery feeling returned.

"Want to dance?" Trevor asked.

Alecia's palms grew damp and her mouth went dry. "I can't dance."

"Come on! It's just one dance." Trevor grabbed her hand and pulled her onto the floor.

Alecia felt like a marionette as she and Trevor moved around the small living room, bumping into other couples, trying to find the rhythm.

"I'm not big on parties but Monica doesn't take no for an answer," Trevor said.

"Monica has a lot of enthusiasm." Alecia wasn't as fond of Monica as Anne, but Trevor's criticism bothered her. "She means well —" Alecia hated how prim and school-teacherish she sounded.

"Yeah, well. Hey, I hear you guys finally won last weekend."

Finally? Why did he have to add that? "Yes, we did. It was a good game."

"That's great. So how long have you been playing soccer?"

"Since I was about seven. How 'bout you?" Alecia concentrated so hard on what she was doing she couldn't relax or enjoy herself. She was convinced everyone in the room was watching her.

"I switched from hockey to soccer when I was about eight. I think my parents were happy to get out of taking me to those early morning practices and sitting in cold rinks."

"At least you play hockey inside where it's dry. That's got to be the worst part of soccer — playing in the rain."

"Try spending half your time with your butt on the ice," Trevor laughed.

Alecia gradually felt herself relax to the music. She got wrapped up in their conversation and forgot to be self-conscious about her dancing. Then Trevor brought up the Burrards again.

"So what do you think your chances are in the championships?" he asked. "Think you can pull it off with Karen in net?"

Alecia shrugged. "Yeah, I think so. We're all playing a lot better now."

"I saw some of your last game — Your defence looked strong. Your strikers are a bit slow to get back though."

"What?" Alecia stopped dancing and glared at Trevor. "Our strikers do their jobs just fine!"

All the good feeling she'd had disappeared.

"I'm just saying they can give more defensive support. You should come out to some of our practices. See how our coach does things. I've got some wicked moves I could show you —"

"What do you know about anything?" she asked, anger swelling inside her, her voice rising as she spoke. "You think you're so great, bragging about how good you are, how good your team is when you're barely winning half your games!"

Trevor's eyes widened behind his glasses and his face grew red. He opened his mouth to answer, but no words came out. A crowd had started to gather around them and someone had turned off the music. Alecia barely noticed Anne push through the crowd to stand beside her.

"I'm so tired of hearing about how awesome you are and how much we could learn from you. Maybe the Mavericks need to come and learn something from the Burrards!"

Anne pulled on Alecia's hand. "Come on. Let's get something to eat, Leesh," she said softly, and Alecia allowed herself to be led away, grateful for the chance to blend into the background.

How could she ever have thought Trevor was nice? He was just an egotistical jerk. She wished she'd never danced with him in the first place. And she wished she hadn't liked it so much.

15

Full Steam Ahead

Monday morning Alecia was alone at her locker when Connor found her.

"That was some argument you and Trevor had Saturday." He leaned against his locker, dropping his overflowing backpack. "Everyone was talking about it after you left."

Alecia slammed her locker door, which promptly swung open and hit her in the shoulder. "We were having a perfectly nice conversation and like always, he ruined it with his stupid comments. What is his problem, anyway?"

"He likes you, Leesh," Connor said and turned to his locker. He shoved the backpack in and held it in place with his foot while he grabbed a couple of books from the top shelf. Then he quickly slammed the door before the mess inside spilled out onto the floor.

"Well, he sure has a funny way of showing it, doesn't he?"

"Come on. He's had a crush on you for weeks — probably since he met you. Don't tell me you didn't notice." Connor waved as he headed off down the hall.

Alecia *had* noticed the way Trevor tried to stand near her whenever they were in a group together, and how he was constantly watching her. But she was trying her hardest to ignore him. She didn't *want* Trevor to like her. She didn't want to like him! Life was so much easier when she and Anne and Connor just hung out. She pursed her lips together and snapped the lock in place.

* * *

Jeremy gathered the team together at soccer practice the next week. "When the league approached me to take over as coach of the Burrards, I was hesitant. But I agreed, and, although we've endured some rough patches this season, I'm glad I did."

He looked at the group before him, cleared his throat and took a sip from his water bottle. "I've enjoyed watching each of you mature as players this season. You've learned some tough lessons. But the Burrards I see before me now are stronger and more committed to their team than ever.

"I see no reason we can't finish well in the finals. You've proven you can deliver when the going gets rough and if you keep focused on playing as a team, I know you'll be fine.

"I'm proud of all of you," Jeremy continued. "Whatever the outcome of this weekend is, it's been my pleasure to coach you this season and I'm looking forward to next year."

The group gathered around him clapped loudly and a few girls stamped their feet. Jeremy smiled a little shyly and blushed but Alecia could tell he was pleased.

* * *

On Saturday morning there was a definite buzz in the air when the girls arrived to play their first game. It had rained throughout the week, leaving a muddy swamp on the field.

"It's going to be a dirty one," Laurie announced with a grimace.

"Gee, do you think?" Alecia asked cheekily.

Laughter and a few groans rose up around her and Alecia grinned. She was pumped and ready for this game despite the dismal weather and nasty field conditions.

The Tornados won the toss and play got underway. Their centre passed to a striker who dribbled up the field before passing off to the centre again. As the centre fought off Nancy and Marnie at midfield, the Tornado striker flew up the right side and was ready for the pass when it came. She took it in full stride and raced toward Karen. Nancy tried to take her but the girl faked her brilliantly. Nancy slid all the way into the end zone, spewing up bits of muddy grass and dirty water as she went.

Karen came out of the net to cut the angle but the girl passed off to a teammate. Nancy got right up and charged back into the play, stripping the ball from the striker and moving it up to Alecia, who dribbled down the field.

At the other end she passed off to Lexi, who fired a shot just over the goalkeeper's head. The girl lunged at the ball just as it crossed the line.

"Great play!" Laurie cried as they all leaped on top of Lexi.

Alecia slapped Lexi on the back — it felt like squeezing a soaking mop. She wrinkled her nose and wiped her hands on her own dirty shorts. "Isn't this disgusting?" she said to Laurie as they ran off the field together.

"I'll say. It's hard to tell who's who — everyone's jerseys are so filthy!" Laurie said, shaking her head. She dug a towel out of her bag, and rubbed her hair and face with it.

Alecia nodded as she watched the players on the field. "You never know, it may work to our advantage eventually," she said with a grin.

* * *

Partway through the second half, Karen caught a shot on goal and punted it out to Allison, who trapped it with her chest and then charged up field.

Just over the centre line the Tornados' captain challenged her but Allison gained possession. As she turned to her left, the other girl shoved at her from behind, sending her thudding to the ground. She landed on her left knee groaning.

The ref held up the yellow card, and Jeremy ran out on the field to help Allison. Slowly, she limped towards the Burrards' bench. Jeremy sent Trina to replace Allison. Alecia could hear Lexi muttering under her breath but said nothing as the ball was dropped between Laurie and a Tornados' player and the game resumed.

Lexi picked off a sloppy pass and charged up the right field. Three Tornado players clogged her path and sent her wide, but a drop pass to Alecia sent the other team scrambling. With the field wide open Alecia charged toward the Tornados' goal.

"Leesh!" Lexi screamed.

Lexi caught Alecia's pass and kicked it toward the goal mouth. The Tornado keeper leapt into the air and tipped the ball with her fingers, sending it out of harm's way. But Laurie was there for the loose ball, and she volleyed it over the prone goal-keeper and into the mesh.

As the rest of the team celebrated the goal, Lexi walked up to the Tornados' captain. Standing very close, she pressed a finger into the girl's jersey.

"That's just the beginning," she said in a menacing whisper. "No one hurts a Burrard and gets away with it."

"Are you threatening me?" the other girl snapped back, although Alecia could hear the fear in her voice.

"Of course not. I'm informing you. And in case you lost count, the score is now 2–0. For us."

* * *

The Burrards left the field, filthy but ecstatic.

"We got 'em!" Lexi cried, dancing around, mud spraying up around her.

"Did you see their goalkeeper's face when Lexi scored that third goal?" Marnie asked. "I thought she was going to quit right there!"

"Well, she'll have a nice, long break now ..." Alecia said, "to think about her career in soccer!"

"Did you hear?" Lexi asked, interrupting the laughter. "The Rocketeers won as well. They creamed the Crusaders three–zip!"

Alecia took a long swallow from her water bottle and then hunted through her bag for her sweatpants. They had lots of time before they played their next game.

"I'm not surprised. Stacie is playing great."

"Well, at least we got rid of the Tornados," Allison muttered. Her leg was up on the bench, an ice pack covering her knee.

"How's it feel?" Alecia asked.

"Okay. Jeremy thinks I'll be able to play the next game. Here come your friends, Leesh," Allison said, nodding across the field.

Alecia turned to see Anne, Connor, Monica, and Trevor approaching. As usual, Monica lost no time before she started talking.

"Hey Leesh! We just caught the last bit. Sorry we're late — I had trouble deciding what to wear! I mean, is it going to be hot today? And what's with those clouds! Of course Trevor and Connor were no help at all!"

When Monica stopped talking, an awkward silence fell over the group. Alecia glanced at Laurie, who was staring at the ground. Connor seemed about to speak when Laurie walked away.

"Well, that was rude," Monica said.

"Monica ..." Anne warned.

"You guys looked great!" Connor said quickly.

"Yeah — your uniforms are the best!" Monica agreed. "I saw some of the other teams' uniforms but none of them were as nice as yours. That one team, what were they thinking? What an ugly shade of green! And what is with the goalkeepers' uniforms?"

Alecia and the others laughed. "The goalkeepers wear bright colours so we can tell them from the other players on the field, Mon. And the uniforms aren't supposed to look good — they're just uniforms."

"Who do you play next?" Anne asked.

"The Spitfires just won their game," Jeremy said, hearing Anne's question. "We play them right after lunch."

16

Showdown

Sunday morning Jeremy met with the team before they played the Crusaders. Everyone was pumped after their wins against the Tornados and the Spitfires.

"Yesterday's play was really solid," he began. "I liked your strong teamwork. Keep it up! The game against the Spitfires was tough and you showed how hard you can fight. Let's carry that over today. The Crusaders are playing well too, so keep your focus!"

Both goalkeepers were playing well. At the end of regulation play, the score was tied 1–1.

In the shootout Laurie ran toward the ball, gaining speed as she approached. The Burrards held their breath. She kicked it up into the blue sky.

"It's going to be high," Alecia whispered to Allison.

And it was. The Burrards were silent until they realized the ball had come down over the line.

"Way to go Laurie!"

The Burrards took the win.

"We did it!" Laurie cried as everyone piled on top of her and Karen. "We made it!"

"Who do we play next?" Rianne asked.

"The Rocketeers," said Jeremy.

The Burrards digested this information slowly. The Rocketeers: their archrivals. Stacie's team.

Before any groans could take over, Laurie disengaged herself from the girls and cleared her throat. "We own this final,"
she said in a strong voice. "And we have a good shot at winning. Don't let Stacie intimidate you! She doesn't like a crowd
in front of the net — it flusters her, remember? Do everything
you can to get under her skin — block her view, talk to each
other, whatever — as long as it's legal! Let's capitalize on her
weaknesses!"

* * *

Unfortunately the Rocketeers had the same game plan. Right
from the beginning it was an aggressive game. The Burrards
knew all of Stacie's secrets, but she knew theirs as well.

Midway through the first half the score was tied at 1–1.

"Go hard, Marnie!" Alecia yelled as the Rocketeers gained
possession of the ball after a brief skirmish. "Get her!"

"Open your eyes Ref! That was a foul if I ever saw one!"
Jeremy yelled. He slapped his hand against his thigh and
resumed his pacing.

Marnie threw a Rocketeer off the ball and passed it hard to
Alecia, who took her time settling the wild pass and assessing
the field.

"Alecia! Left!" Allison screamed, and Alecia moved side-
ways, just avoiding a hard check from the advancing defender.
As Allison got open she hit Alecia with a pass and ran in, joining the crowd collecting in front of Stacie.

"Get out of my way!" she cried at a teammate who crossed
the line. Flushing deep red, the Rocketeer moved away.

Alecia looked up and saw the frustrated scowl on Stacie's

face. The Burrards were throwing her off her game! Four were in close, three more just behind the play, and a mess of Rocketeer girls were fighting hard to win back possession. Stacie ran a hand through her short blond hair. She looked totally frazzled. The Burrards were dictating the play.

The half ended with the Rocketeers ahead by one goal. The Burrards had poured on the pressure, but giving so much to their attack had allowed the Rocketeers to burn them on a break-out rush from centre field. The Burrards sat on their bench huddled in their jackets, already feeling defeated; Karen most of all.

"I didn't see it coming! I'm sorry, guys. I wasn't paying attention."

"Karen, stop it," Jeremy said. "They're a good team. They're going to score some. You've done a great job and we're still in this game. Just don't lose your focus."

"We can't come this far and lose," Laurie told them. "We came in second at the last tournament and that was big for us. But we're not settling for second place this time — RIGHT?"

"RIGHT!" the team yelled in answer.

* * *

Alecia bent over, hands on knees, and took several deep breaths. The play had speeded up in the second half. It hadn't seemed possible, but they were dirtier now than they had been in the last mudbath and it was getting hard to identify teammates.

The play moved right in front of her, a Rocketeer driving past. Alecia tore after her and slid into her, tipping the ball away from the other girl. It rolled through the muck and Laurie picked it up.

The Rocketeers were caught out of position — and Laurie

had a wide-open field. Trina joined her, and the two girls advanced up the field using give-and-go passes. As they neared the net, Lexi snuck up on the right side. Twenty feet from the goal she charged in, took a sliding pass from Trina, and rocketed the ball past Stacie into the net. Tie game.

The noise from the field and the bench was deafening. Trina and Lexi were engulfed in a sea of arms as the team swarmed them.

"YES!" Jeremy yelled from the sidelines. "Great job girls!"

The winning goal came with thirty seconds left in regulation time, off a bad play. The Rocketeers' centre had possession of the ball. She looked up, saw hands waving and, exhausted, made a clumsy desperation pass to a mud-covered Burrard.

Too late, she realized her mistake. Laurie charged the centre line, Allison joining her on the rush. Alecia ran after the play, her thoughts racing.

Stacie was a great goalkeeper. If Laurie missed the net and they went to a shoot out, well, she didn't even want to think about that possibility.

Everything seemed to slow down as Laurie and Allison got closer and closer to Stacie. All around her, Alecia could feel the tension of her teammates as they watched Laurie set up for the shot. Allison leaned in and kicked the ball. It went right over Laurie's head. Confused, Stacie stumbled and as she hesitated, Lexi headed the ball over Stacie's shoulder and into the back of the net. The score was 3–2.

Screams erupted on the field as their teammates piled on top of Lexi, Laurie and Allison. They did it!

"We won!" cried Alecia in disbelief. "We won the finals!"

Finally the Burrards untangled themselves, still laughing and hugging each other. As Alecia stood up she caught sight of Stacie, standing alone in her net, watching them. They looked at each other for several seconds. Alecia felt a slight twinge of pity, but when she started to speak Stacie ran off, so Alecia turned back to her teammates.

Jeremy, Mrs. Parker and several other parents ran out on the field. Alecia threw herself into Jeremy's arms, nearly knocking him off balance.

"We did it Dad! Can you believe it? We won!" she cried, still jubilant.

"We did it, Leesh," he said, and hugged her close.

17

Champions

"Congratulations," Trevor said on Monday morning.

Alecia spun around and smiled at him.

"Thanks! It was so amazing!" she began but then stopped, remembering that Trevor's team had been eliminated in the first round.

"Yeah, it was. You girls played great."

"You were there? Really?" Warmth spread through Alecia and she blushed.

"Sure. Anyway, I wanted to apologize for what I said at Monica's. Sometimes I say stuff that's kind of dumb."

"Yeah, well ... thanks," Alecia sputtered.

"Sometimes I start to say something and it comes out wrong, you know? Then it's too late."

"Me too. Just ask Connor."

"My mom is always telling me to stop and think before I speak—"

"My mother says the same thing."

They smiled shyly at each other. Then they both started speaking at the same time.

"I was wondering if ..."

"A bunch of us are ..."

"Sorry, you go ahead," Alecia told him.

"Well, I thought some of your plays last weekend were really cool. I wondered if you'd maybe, you know, show them to me sometime?"

At first Alecia wasn't sure if she'd heard right. Was Trevor asking her for soccer help? Slowly she nodded, surprising herself as she said, "Yeah, sure. A bunch of us are getting together Saturday morning to kick the ball around. You can join us then if you want." She couldn't believe she'd actually said it! She forced herself to just act normal.

"Sure, that sounds good."

"We're meeting at the field by the school around ten."

"I'll try to keep my mouth shut," he said, blushing.

"It's okay. Thanks for apologizing." Alecia smiled and tucked a piece of hair behind her ear.

* * *

Alecia arrived before the others on Saturday morning, anxious. She kept glancing around the field, watching.

"Hey, you're here early."

Laurie dropped her bag down on the bench. She was dressed in their team jersey, shorts and socks, with her hair tied back in a ponytail. Over her shoulder, Alecia noticed a tall skinny boy with black hair and wire-rimmed glasses standing by himself.

"Is that Ethan?"

"Yes." Laurie blushed. "Is it okay if he watches? He really likes soccer. He's been helping me practise."

"Practise — for what? The season is over."

"Well, I've decided to audition for the Premier League. Try-outs are next month."

"But if you make it you'll have to quit the Burrards." Alecia's heart sank.

"Yeah, I know. But I was going to resign as captain anyway. I'm not a good captain. I'm not tough enough and my feelings get hurt too easily."

Alecia started to object but Laurie held up her hand. Maybe Laurie was right.

"Well, Anne's decided to come back — maybe she'll be captain again," Alecia said, thinking out loud.

"Actually, Jeremy and I talked about it, and we think you should be captain." Laurie looked at Alecia with raised eyebrows.

"Me? I don't know ..." Sudden panic overwhelmed Alecia.

"Alecia, you're a strong player and all the other girls like you. You'll be great."

"Lots of other girls would be better! Sometimes I say the wrong thing and I'm always complaining."

Laurie laughed and shook her head. "You don't always complain — just when it rains! And besides, you don't have to be perfect. Look at me! Oh, there's Anne, I need to talk to her."

Alecia stared at Laurie. Captain? Her? Were they crazy? Still, she was flattered ... Her brain began to fill with ideas. She smiled and shook her head.

Alecia reached into her bag and pulled out her cleats. She'd have to get new shoes for next season she thought, examining the worn toes.

Laurie's words rang in Alecia's head. If Jeremy hadn't refused to let her quit, Alecia wouldn't have the trophy and gold medal sitting on the mantel at home, nor would she have been asked to be captain next year.

"This is going to be fun!" Anne dropped down on the bench beside Alecia. Her cheeks were flushed.

"Yeah, I think so. I'm glad you're coming back next season, Annie."

"Yeah, me too. Tyler convinced me, actually. He's big on exercise," she said, laughing. "What were you and Laurie talking about before?"

"Oh, well, Laurie is going to try for the Premier League. And apparently I'm going to be captain of the Burrards."

"Alecia, that's so great!" Anne threw her arms around Alecia. "Who'd have thought?" she teased and Alecia laughed.

"Not me, that's for sure." She turned. "Hey Connor. Are you here to play?"

"Yeah, right. Make room, I'm coming down." Connor squeezed between the two girls and put an arm around each of them. Slowly the old Connor was returning.

"Alecia's going to be captain of the Burrards next season, Connor," Anne said. "Isn't that awesome?"

"It is. And I heard she's going on a date."

"I'm not going on a date! Is that what Trevor told you?" Alecia cried.

"He said you asked him to come play today …"

"That's not a date, Connor —" Alecia told him, but she blushed as she spoke.

"Well, I'm glad you changed your mind about him, anyway. He's a nice guy."

"I know."

"It's funny, when you think back to last August when you were whining about starting grade eight, whining about Jeremy coaching the Burrards, and …" Connor flinched as Alecia punched his arm.

"Can't whine about Jeremy coaching anymore!" Anne cried, laughing. "I just wish I'd been out there playing with you guys. It was so amazing! And Alecia, really, next year will be even better."

"Even with all these new changes, Leesh? We all know how

much you hate change after all ..." Connor teased.

Alecia looked up at the clear blue sky and closed her eyes. The spring sun warmed her face and she smiled. The old sense of dread she'd felt whenever things changed had slowly been replaced with anticipation. Who knew what was around the corner? She opened her eyes and smiled at her friends.

"Oh well, things change," she said. "That's life."

Other books you'll enjoy in the Sports Stories series

Soccer

❏ *Alecia's Challenge* by Sandra Diersch #32
Thirteen-year-old Alecia has to cope with a new school, a new step-father, and friends who have suddenly discovered the opposite sex.

❏ *Offside!* by Sandra Diersch #43
Alecia has to confront a new girl who drives her teammates crazy.

❏ *Heads Up!* by Dawn Hunter and Karen Hunter #45
Do the Warriors really need a new, hot-shot player who skips practice?

❏ *Off the Wall* by Camilla Reghelini Rivers #52
Lizzie loves indoor soccer, and she's thrilled when her little sister gets into the sport. But when their teams are pitted against each other, Lizzie can only warn her sister to watch out.

❏ *Trapped!* by Michele Martin Bossley #53
There's a thief on Jane's soccer team, and everyone thinks it's her best friend, Ashley. Jane must find the true culprit to save both Ashley and the team's morale.

❏ *Soccer Star!* by Jacqueline Guest #61
Samantha longs to show up Carly, the school's reigning soccer star, but her new interest in theatre is taking up a lot of her time. Can she really do it all?

❏ *Miss Little's Losers* by Robert Rayner #64
The Brunswick Valley School soccer team haven't won a game all season long. When their coach resigns, the only person who will coach them is Miss Little … their former kindergarten teacher!

❏ *Just for Kicks* by Robert Rayner #69
When their parents begin taking their games too seriously, it's up to the soccer-mad gang from Brunswick Valley School to reclaim the spirit of their sport.